HOUNDED!

By Justine Korman

Illustrated by Animated Arts

A GOLDEN BOOK • NEW YORK
Western Publishing Company, Inc., Racine, Wisconsin 53404

ANIMANIACS, characters, names, and all related indicia are trademarks of Warner Bros. © 1994. W89. All rights reserved. Printed in the U.S.A. No part of this book may be reproduced or copied in any form without written permission from the copyright owner. All other trademarks are the property of Western Publishing Company, Inc. Library of Congress Catalog Card Number: 94-76311 ISBN: 0-307-12839-3/ISBN: 0-307-62839-6 (lib. bdg.)   A MCMXCIV

One day three wacky characters escaped from the Warner Bros. film studio. They were Yakko, Wakko, and Dot Warner—two brothers and a sister, looking for excitement.

Ralph, the security guard, chased the trio down
Main Street, blowing his whistle and waving his arms.
"We have to get away from him!" said Yakko,
panting hard. "We need to find a place to hide."

Yakko stopped running so suddenly that his brother and sister plowed into him. Then he pointed to a HELP WANTED sign in front of a fancy dog hotel.

"Good!" said Wakko. "Since this isn't the right time for my new rainy-day getaway trick, let's take the job to get away from Ralph."

When the Warners rushed into the hotel lobby, the manager said, "Good morning! Have you come about the job?"

"Yes, siree," said Wakko. "We're the Warner brothers and sister Dot!"

Mr. Barker showed the Warners around the hotel. Then he asked for references.

"Right here!" said Wakko, taking some letters from the sack of magic tricks he always carried.

"Well . . . these references *are* good," Mr. Barker said. "The job is to look after these prize pooches—to feed, walk, and bathe the dogs . . ."

"We'll take it," interrupted Wakko. "When's lunch?"

"Actually, it's time for me to go to breakfast," Mr. Barker said as he took the Warners into the kitchen. "And schedules must be maintained! Here is each dog's menu, and there are the supplies you'll need."

When he was gone, Dot opened a can of dog food. It smelled so terrible that she and her brothers decided to order pizza instead.

While Dot let the dogs out of their kennels, Wakko opened the pizzas. Within minutes the Canine Castle was rocking with a wild pizza party!

The "guests" were having a great time. One of the
dogs kept Yakko busy with a lively game of Frisbee,
while another pup played tug-of-cheese with Wakko.
Dot entertained them all with her juggling skills.

When Mr. Barker returned, he was furious. "Clean up this mess!" he howled. Then he looked at his watch. "Oh, no! It's time for *walkies*, and after that a bubble bath for each guest."

"Relax," Wakko said. "We'll handle the walkies and the baths."

"All right," said Mr. Barker. "One more chance."

The Warners headed down the street with the dogs.
"I wonder if my flower's on straight," said Dot.

"I wonder if your head's on straight," said Yakko.

"I wonder how we're going to finish walkies and
baths—*and* stay away from Ralph!" said Wakko.

Yakko snapped his fingers. "Look!" he cried. "We
can do everything at the same time—in a car wash!"

The dogs were so excited to be outdoors, they were ready to go anywhere—even into the car wash!

On the way inside, Wakko pulled shower caps and shampoo from his wacky sack and passed the supplies to his brother and sister.

Inside, the trio helped the dogs onto the moving conveyor. An attendant arrived just in time to see a quartet of dogs gliding through the car wash in mid-shampoo.

"What's going on here?" the attendant demanded.

Before he could get an answer, the dogs were washed and rinsed and headed for the buffers.

The twirling strands of buffing cloth gave Dot an idea. "Follow the leader!" she cried. "Get in line for a shiny coat."

Everyone formed a swaying line behind Dot, and they hula-danced through the flipping chamois strips.

Then Dot dried the dogs and fluffed their fur.
Once they were finished, the dogs and their
handlers had no choice but to leave the car wash.
Yakko looked outside to see if Ralph was in sight.
The coast was clear, so they ran to a nearby park.

When they were in the park, Dot gave the dogs one last look. Something was missing. "I know!" she said at last. "These dogs need some fashionable fur cuts."

"For fur cuts, you need fur cutters," said Wakko as he pulled clippers of all sizes from his sack.

In a jiffy Dot trimmed all the dogs in her own special style.

Dot put a flower on her last customer. "There!
Don't the doggies look beautiful?" she said proudly.
    "Swell," Yakko agreed. "But we'd better put the
leashes on the dogs and get back to the hotel." He
imitated Mr. Barker's snooty voice. "Schedules must
be maintained."

"Not so fast!" said Wakko, taking a camera from
his sack. "These gorgeous pups are front-page news!
If they don't make the cover of *Dogs Illustrated*,
nothing will!"

When the Warners and their charges approached
the hotel, Mr. Barker stopped them before they
could get inside. "What have you done!" he shrieked
when he saw the stylish hounds. "I'm ruined! You're
fired," Mr. Barker screamed hysterically.

"And don't ever come back," Mr. Barker yelled, grabbing the dogs' leashes.

The dogs barked as the Warners sadly walked away.

Just then several of the dog owners approached the hotel.

To Mr. Barker's surprise, the dog owners *loved* how their pooches looked. "Oh, Boopsie's beautiful!" one cooed.

"I've never seen our Pickles look perkier!" another marveled.

"It's a new service we're offering," Mr. Barker explained hastily. "I guess I was wrong about you," he said to the Warners. "Won't you please stay?"

At that moment Yakko spotted Ralph coming down the block. "Wakko!" he cried just as it started to rain. "The time is right for the rainy-day getaway."

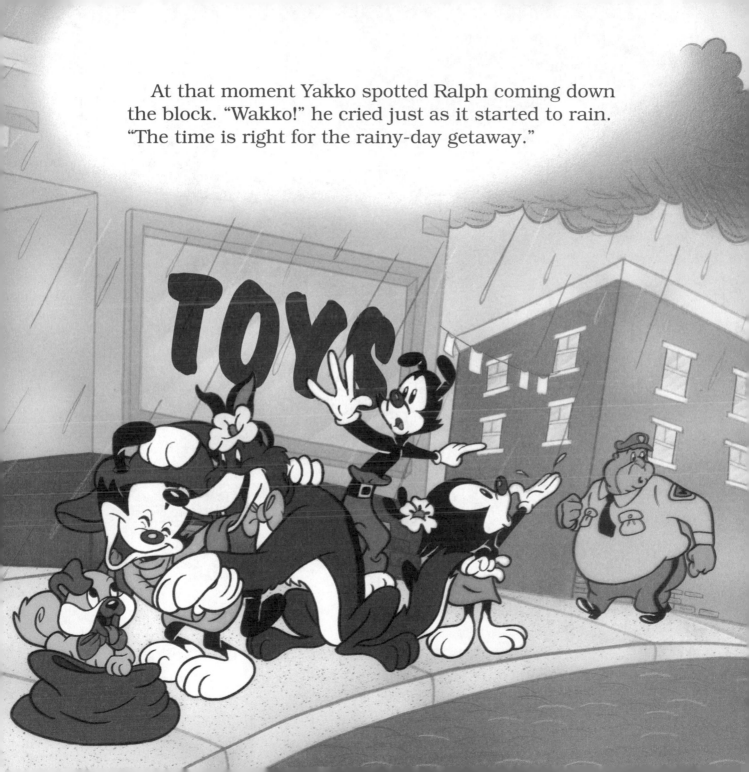

"We've got to fly!" said Wakko, pulling a magic umbrella out of his bag. And while Ralph raged in the street below, the Warners flew up, up, and away! "Sorry, Ralph," called Dot. "Better luck next time!"